THE ADVENTURES

OF

GORDON THE GREYHOUND

by

MICK WHEBLE

Published in 2004

By

KISMET PUBLISHING COMPANY LIMITED

UK

4 6 7 6 3 7 4

ISBN 0-9544769-2-1

Printed and bound in the United Kingdom

By
Cox & Wyman
Reading

Illustrated by A J Green

Edited by J Willson

This book is dedicated to the following people -

My devoted parents, Ethel Emily and James. They were my inspiration and simply the best parents I could ever have wished for. I miss them deeply.

My darling granddaughter, Rachel Kathleen Jordan Wheble, who is the apple of my eye, my two wonderful sisters, Carol and Marlene, Jimmy my brother, all my supportive in-laws who all in all help make up a very close knit family.

Not forgetting of course my beautiful wife Kathleen and my terrific son Jeffrey.

Kind thanks to
Richard Dunn of RD Racing
Who has been a great help to me in producing this story.

And
A big thank you to
My Publishers
For their help and dedication in getting this book published.
www.kismetpublishers.com

THE ADVENTURES
OF
GORDON THE GREYHOUND

"Hello. My name is Gordon. Gordon the Greyhound. I look like a greyhound, in fact a very handsome black greyhound, if I say so myself. I run like a greyhound. I even smell like a greyhound. But I'm not like any other greyhound you would know.

Yes, I can run as fast as the wind and winning races is a piece of cake, but as far as my master is concerned I have one big, big problem!

THE BEGINNING

I can remember when I was just a pup. The sweet smell of my mother's milk and the warmth of her as I nuzzled into her tummy. The world was dark to begin with but this didn't bother me. I felt safe when curled up against my mother.

Gradually the darkness turned to a bluish haze until one morning I awoke to a blinding glare. The brightness hurt my eyes, I blinked once, and then twice, I didn't much like the brightness, so I shut my eyes tightly to stop them hurting.

Just like any youngster, it wasn't long before curiosity got the better of me. I opened my eyes again and looked around me for the first time. I soon realised that the warm, wriggly objects that had continually pushed me away from my food at the start of my life, were actually just like me, although different colours. My mother was so beautiful, her fur was a dark brindle, as soft as silk. It was wonderful to see where that delicious smell of milk came from. Let's face it when you are only a week or so old that is all you are interested in.

I kept blinking and staring at my mum, she smiled then bent to gently lick me, and her big blue eyes twinkled as she said.

"My, my. Look at my baby. You have eyes the colour of amber just like your father. He was such a handsome greyhound, black as the night and as fast as the wind, a champion of greyhounds. You will be just like him Gordon, I can see it now."

Wow! I was going to be just like my dad. He sounded like a great greyhound. I would have to do my best to be just like him.

Mum would often tell us pups off; we were always getting into bother. If we didn't take any notice of her, she would grab us by the scruff of our necks and shake us gently.

"Now, now children, stop your squabbling."

Mum never hurt us, we knew when she was cross though, and it was always best to do as we were told. Well, for five minutes anyway!

There was hardly a quiet moment in this place where I lived, there was always the sound of barking echoing from somewhere. The noise was something that I had got used to since the day I was born. My mother had told me there were loads more families just like ours in this place, called kennels. It was very funny to hear other pups being told off by their mums, so I wasn't so unusual after all.

As time went on, I became more and more aware of my surroundings, often leaving my mothers side, but not her ever-watchful eye. It was great fun with my brothers and sisters, tumbling about, grabbing each other's ears, and nipping at feet with little sharp teeth. There were quite a few yelps ringing about the kennel, I can tell you. The nipping bit wasn't very nice, it hurt, but us pups were still learning. However, I learnt a lot quicker than my brothers and sisters, I soon realised I didn't like getting nipped. I didn't want to hurt them either, so I stopped playing this nasty game. However, my brothers and sisters didn't, and they couldn't understand why I wouldn't join in the pretend battles. They made so much fun of me and called me names.

"Yellow belly."

"Nah, Nah. Who's a big softy?"

I suppose I should have realised then that I was different to other greyhounds but I didn't, instead I cuddled up to my mum who reassured me.

"Take no notice of them son. You will be ok. Some things take time."

"What things?" I thought, and then the question went out of mind as something more important happened. I had an itch and it needed scratching badly.

It wasn't long before the rest of my family got tired with their games and scurried back to mum, nestling once again into her warmth and to the comfort of her long sweeping tongue that licked each one of us from head to claw. She soon got us off to sleep.

It had felt so safe curled up against my mother with the constant shoving and bickering of my brothers and sisters that it came as quite a shock when one by one they were taken away. In the end there was just my mum, my sister Sophie and I left.

GORDON WITH
HIS BROTHERS
& SISTERS

It was of course much easier to get food, but the fact that my family was getting smaller by the day was quite scary. What was happening to them all?

The worst was yet to come; my mother went out for her usual walk with the Wellington boot man and never came back. Of course Sophie and I cried for a days, but the man came to feed us and talked to us, he was very kind. We soon came to realise that our mother was never coming back. We were now old enough to look after ourselves.

THE MAN

The door to our kennel opened and the man with the Wellington boots came in.

"Hello Gordon, hello Sophie."

He tried to lay two bowls of food on the floor, we were so hungry we tried to get to them scratching at the Wellington boots and nudging the bowls as they got near enough.

"Hold on you two. You'll make me spill it." He made that funny noise that humans make, we knew he thought we were funny. The food was put on the ground and the nice man left. I managed to get my foot in the bowl. It was a bit messy but it kept the bowl still. Sophie and I were very hungry so we gobbled it up, not leaving a scrap.

I had eaten so fast I had hiccups and Sophie laughed at me and jumped up and down on my back to try and get me to stop. We wore ourselves out with our antics and lay on the hay and had almost gone to sleep when we heard the sound of footsteps. I recognised those of the Wellington boot man, but there was also some more that I hadn't heard before.

Our kennel door opened, the Wellington boot man came in followed by another man. Who was he? I ran to check him out, followed by Sophie. Before we knew it ropes were put around our necks and we were being tugged by them. We both dug our heels into the ground, we didn't like these things around our necks. The Wellington boot man stooped down and picked up Sophie.

"Come on you little devil, we are going for a walk."

I was scooped up by the strange man. He didn't hurt me, it was certainly better than being pulled along.

We were taken past the other kennels and for the first time I saw all the other families.

"Hello." I shouted.

Everyone answered, the noise was deafening. A large white greyhound called after us.

"Do as you are told and you will be ok. Don't be frightened."

Once outside we were put on the ground and the men started to walk, they tugged at the ropes and remembering what the white greyhound had said we followed. He was right, it was ok. It was good to get out of the kennel for the first time, this was quite an adventure.

The noise from the cars and lorries seemed to pierce my ears and the flashing lights coming from them made me jump.

"It's okay little fella." The man said as he bent and patted me. "I won't let anything happen to you."

Well that was nice to know. I could now sniff out the territory and look at the other humans. Some had little humans with them and others had dogs, none of these dogs looked like Sophie and I though. It was all very new and strange.

"Think that's enough for today don't you Sid?" Sid was the man holding my rope.

"Yep. We don't want to wear the littleuns out."

I didn't really want to go back as I was wanted to know more about the world about me. It had been quite a day though and the excitement had worn both of us out so reluctantly we were led back to our kennels. We immediately went back to our bed of hay, two little worn out souls.

It felt as though I had just fallen asleep when I was awoken by excited yapping and barking from the other greyhounds and the sound of the Wellington boots came nearer. The door opened.

"Hello you two, its dinnertime, now take it easy I don't want this all over me."

Both of us were still sleepy eyed and had stayed on our bed, but at the word dinnertime our ears pricked up and when two bowls were put on the ground we didn't hesitate and bounded over to them.

"Soup for you tonight, I want to see nice clean bowls when I come back."

We didn't need telling twice, we lapped up the soup of meat and green vegetables – it was very tasty. Even when it had all gone we went to each other's bowls just to make sure that nothing had been left. We even used our noses to lift the bowls to see if there was anything underneath, it was disappointing to find that it had definitely all gone. We were growing fast, there never did seem to be enough food and after satisfying ourselves that there wasn't anymore, we settled down on the hay once more, snuggling against each other to keep warm. The kennel got darker and quieter – it was time to sleep, we closed our eyes and drifted off. The day had ended.

**GORDON
AND SOPHIE**

THE NEXT FEW WEEKS

As time passed I grew bigger and stronger. Now I had longer legs I could leap onto my bed in one jump instead of having to scramble up the side.

One morning a strange thing happened, something that was going to change my life forever. The man with the Wellington boots came as usual with our breakfast, but this time he had another man with him. I recognised him from somewhere.

"Well Sid, have you decided then?"

That's it. I remembered who he was. He was the man that took me on my first walk. I wondered what he wanted.

"I'll have that one" I heard him say, pointing at me. "Not the white one, I definitely want this black one."

"OK Sid. Wise choice. He's going to be a champion that one."

"Just tell me where to sign."

"Come this way."

The men left us and all was quiet once again. Just as I was about to fall asleep, Sophie suddenly snarled. I looked up, her ears were pricked, and tail up as she continued snarling like a mad dog. She skidded across the kennel floor and went headfirst into the bars, landing in a heap.

"Ouch!"

"What are you doing?" I asked.

"Didn't you see that mouse?" Sophie said as she scrambled to her feet.

"Yes I did. So What?"

"Well, why didn't you chase it and bite it – you're faster than me and you could have caught it."

"Why would I want to do that? That mouse was only looking for crumbs to eat – it wasn't doing us any harm."

"That's not the point. We're greyhounds, we are supposed to chase and kill anything furry, they are our enemies."

"They're not *my* enemies. Why should I want to hurt furry animals, after all they done nothing to harm me?"

"Well someone's in for a surprise. When they take you home and you don't want to chase and kill, you'll be kicked out of your kennel."

The next day the Wellington boot man came earlier than usual with our breakfast, he had Sid with him.

"There you go Sid. He's all yours now."

The next thing I knew there was a collar being put around my neck and before I had time to say goodbye to Sophie I had been carried from the kennel and loaded into a tin truck. The doors slammed shut behind me and I was left in semi-darkness. After a short while of being in the truck, battered by the bumpy ride and deafened by the noise of the engine, the truck came to a halt. The doors opened, I didn't know where I was. Sid attached a lead to the collar he had put on me earlier.

"Right Gordon, this is your new home. You are going to run like the wind, be faster than an aeroplane and make me lots and lots of money."

I looked around as I walked along the pathway; there were hundreds of trees and acres of grass. It looked a nice place, Sophie and I could have had some good times here. Dear Sophie I was missing her already.

We walked up to some huge gates, Sid pulled at them. CLANG, CLANG, SCREECH was the noise they made as they were pulled open. We went through them, I was very wary of these noisy gates, I kept my eye on them, just in case they decided to chase me.

Sid took me into a strange kennel, it didn't smell like my home. There was another human in the kennel, shorter than Sid but a little wider, this person was filling a shiny silver bowl with water.

"Just getting Gordon's new home ready."

"Hello darling, you've made it nice and cosy for him." Sid said.

"Darling" knelt down beside me and patted my head saying - "He's a real beauty Sid – a champion if ever I saw one."

Gently holding my head *"Darling"* looked me in the eye. "Now you be a good little boy Gordon and we will see you in the morning."

"See you in the morning Gordon – we'll have you training in no time."

SLAM went the door – I was left, frightened and alone in this strange place that was my new home. At least it was warm and dry. I curled up on the dry hay and soon drifted into a deep sleep, where I dreamt of Sophie and my mum, who I was never to see again.

GORDON'S
NEW HOME

THE NEXT MORNING

I awoke to the sound of dogs barking, but it was different, not what I had been used to. Then suddenly the kennel door burst open and Sid appeared.

"Right Gordon. It's time for you to start training to be that champion."

Once again I was led passed kennels where there were other greyhounds. These ones didn't shout out to me though, but I could hear them whispering as I went passed.

"That's the new one."

"Yes, heard his father was a world champion."

"Let's hope he doesn't disappoint the master then."

I was put into the tin truck and after a short journey, arrived at a weird place. It was a circular area covered in sand there was a fence all around it. Could it be the seaside that I had heard of. If so this could be fun. I tugged at the lead I wanted to run on the sand.

"Hold on Gordon. You'll get your chance in a minute." Sid said, trying to calm me down.

Then in the distance I spotted lots of greyhounds, like me but with different colouring. I got excited, wondering if Sophie was here or maybe my mother or other brothers and sisters – I had not seen them all for such a long time. I gazed around but became sad when I realised they were not there – I tried not to whimper, but it was hard and every so often a little one would slip out.

"Right Gordon – come here." Sid bent down and put this cover made of wire over my mouth, I didn't like it. It was horrid. Where was I going? What was happening to me?

Two other greyhounds joined me. They looked at me, both had wire covers over their mouths to. This was most odd. Maybe this was a game and we were going to play and have fun.

I was lost in my thoughts when without warning I was bundled into a very cramped box. I could see out of it but could not turn around and the bars stopped me from leaving. I was well and truly trapped once the door had

27

shut behind me. Then a loud whirring noise sounded in my ears, I thought I was going to come to a sticky end and was beginning to panic. I started to scratch at the barred window when like magic it crashed opened, I must have hit the right button. I could see daylight again, looking to my right a white and brown furry object flashed past. On my left were the two greyhounds I saw earlier. They started to run really fast. So this was the game. I can catch them. Within seconds I caught up with my two strange friends.

"Hello kid" said the one next to me. "Go on run, you are younger than us, try and catch the hare."

So that was the white thing bouncing and bobbing in front of me. I was curious why the hare was running so fast, I wanted to catch it and ask him. I ran faster and faster, then like magic the furry object disappeared down a hole. I stood there bewildered – where had it gone? I looked down the hole where it had gone. He was nowhere to be seen. I was still panting when Sid came and put the lead around my neck.

GORDON'S FIRST TRIAL RUN

"Well done Gordon, you made them other two dogs look like snails – good boy!" I felt ever so proud my master was pleased with me.

Sid led me to what looked like a small garden with a hedge all around it. I could not get out. He turned to another man who had just joined him. "I told you he was a champion, did you see him run? He beat those other two hounds by a mile – he can run as fast as a sports car."

"Yes, but is he keen enough? Is he savage enough?"

"Of course he is. He's a greyhound – watch this and I'll prove it to you."

Sid put his hand into a sack and pulled out a fluffy brown, one-eyed, one-eared rabbit and threw it to the ground and said "Go on Gordon – attack, attack. Kill that rabbit!"

The rabbit was running around frantically trying to escape. *"Why should I want to attack this rabbit, he hadn't done anything to me, he hasn't frightened me – he's a nice little thing"* I thought.

Sid continued to urge me on. "Go on Gordon, what are you waiting for attack, attack, bite him, bite him." Sid pushed me towards the rabbit but I just couldn't bring myself to chase it, let alone bite the poor thing. It was so frightened.

"Told you. He's not got that nasty streak Sid – he may be able to run fast but he just hasn't got that 'killer instinct' – bring him back to me when he's killed a rabbit. Until then he's not much use as a racing greyhound."

While this conversation was going on, the big fluffy one-eyed, one eared rabbit had found a hole in the fence and escaped. I was so pleased and relieved that he had escaped, he looked as though he had already had a bad time of things. He was free at last, I was not so lucky!

"You coward" shouted Sid angrily. "You are no good to me, you're useless."

I saw him undo his belt and before I could move out of the way he had lifted it into the air and brought it down heavily across my back. I yelped with the pain, I had never been hit before. I felt shocked and frightened.

"You useless dog. There will be no dinner for you tonight or any other night until you catch and kill a rabbit or a hare. You'd better do what I say tomorrow or else you will feel my belt again" Sid then put the lead around my neck and dragged me towards the truck, he picked me up and threw me in and when we got back to the kennel he left me with no food or water. I lay cowering on my bed, my back was sore. I was so sad, cold and hungry. What was I to do? I could never be horrible to the furry creatures – it just wasn't in my nature. I knew the only thing left for me to do was to run away. I would try and find my family who loved and looked after me. How could I get out of my kennel? The door was locked – I tried scratching at the sides to see if I could make a hole but it was too hard and this made my paws hurt. I had to think of another plan to escape the evil Sid.

THE ESCAPE

I could not sleep all night. I was racking my brains to think of how to get away from this kennel and my owners. Then it came to me – I knew that when Sid opened the kennel door in the morning, he would leave the main door to the house open as well. If I could just slip past him, through the house and jump the wall I would be free! I kept awake for the rest of the night pacing up and down nervously. It was dark and quiet and I could hear rain falling and the trees rustling in the breeze. It seemed as if the night would never end. Then as it got lighter I heard the movements of the other dogs beginning to awaken. I knew it was nearly time for Sid to come trundling up the path towards my kennel. "*Concentrate*" I thought to myself "*You will only get one chance to escape to freedom*" I was scared, like a coiled spring waiting to unwind. After all, if I missed this chance, my life would be made hell.

BANG the noise of the first door opening and hitting the wall. The other greyhounds were barking in anticipation of their first meal of the day. Sid's footsteps were coming nearer. I held my breath. He had now stopped outside my door. I lay in wait ready to spring forward as the door opened. The key turned, the door slowly opened, just as Sid's boots appeared I seized my chance. I ran like the wind towards the open door, brushing past Sid, who had turned and was now chasing after me.

"Oi, where do you think you're going. Gordon, come back here you useless bag of bones."

I didn't look back only forward, the light of the sky was shining through the open door ahead beckoning me towards it and freedom. The other greyhounds were cheering me on.

"Go on Gordon lad."

"Good on you Gordon."

I made it through the door then skidded sideways, my back legs losing their grip on the damp path, seeming to move like a snail for a few seconds and not a forty mile an hour greyhound. Somehow I managed to regain my steps, the wall loomed up in front of me, and taking a deep breath, clenching my teeth I leapt as high as I could. It was easy, my long legs hadn't let me down. I was now on the soft grass outside the kennels. Now I would be able to grip much more easily. I could hear Sid's angry voice getting fainter as I ran and ran through open land and fields putting as much distance between us as I could.

I ran for miles until I reached some woodland when I had to slow down. My feet were beginning to get sore and my legs starting to ache. I had run from the early morning and now it was getting dark. The bird song was getting weaker as it was time for them to sleep. I just could not run anymore, I was exhausted!

My heart was pounding with fright and I wondered if I were far enough away not to get caught. If I was caught there was no telling what Sid would do to me. Then I remembered that I was black and as it was night time it would be hard for anyone to see me. How I wished it would stay dark forever, then no-one would be able to see me and catch me ever again. Now I had stopped running, a shiver ran down my spine, it was getting cold. There was a dense growth of trees nearby so that's where I decided I would rest. I nestled down under them, curling my body round and went to sleep, one scared but free greyhound.

DURING THE NIGHT

A rustling noise was disturbing me. I was so tired, I didn't move to find out what was causing it. Seconds later there was a loud "SNAP" like that of a twig being stood upon. Now I had to look up to see what it was. Imagine my surprise when I found beside me a carrot, green leaves and some bread. I was so hungry, this was just what I needed to get my strength back. I gobbled the whole lot down, not stopping to wonder where it had come from.

I could see the stars twinkling intermittently between the moving leaves of the trees. There were two big yellow stars between the tree trunks. All of a sudden they disappeared, then as quickly as they went, they came back again, like the beam of a torch going on and off.

"Hang on." I said to myself. "I don't think they are stars at all." "Hello. Is anyone there?" I asked nervously. There was no answer. "I know someone is there – won't you talk to me." Then a warm voice answered.

"I am Fergal the fox – I brought you the food."

"Thank you. I was so hungry. Won't you come and join me?"

"I don't know about that. I've heard about you greyhounds. You are not supposed to like us foxes – you might try and bite me."

"Of course I won't – I'm not like other greyhounds. I like all animals – foxes, hares, rabbits, and mice. I like ALL of you."

"How do I know you're telling the truth?" said Fergal.

"Because I am the fastest animal on earth – except of course for the cheetah – and I could easily have chased you and caught you if I had wanted to."

"I suppose you're right" Fergal replied appearing from behind a tree. "Whats your name and why are you here?"

"My name is Gordon and I ran away from home because my master wanted me to chase a one-eyed, one eared fluffy rabbit, but because I didn't want to hurt him my master beat me and that is why I ran away."

"Your master will be looking for you as greyhounds are valuable. It'll be hard for him to find you in these woods and fields though. I will show you where the safest places are to hide."

"Does that mean we are friends Fergal?"

"Yes Gordon. But you must try and understand it will not be easy for you to make friends here. You are a greyhound and most of my friends are small and furry – you're supposed to chase, catch and hurt us – they will be scared of you."

"But Fergal I have no wish to harm them. I want to be friends with all of them."

"Follow me Gordon, while it is still dark. Your coat is so black it will be hard for any human to see you."

As we wandered through the woods Fergal asked me about the rabbit, I should have killed.

"Did you say that the rabbit only had one eye?"

"Yes"

"Did you say he only had one ear as well?"

"Yes."

"And you say you let him go?"

"Yes, I could have easily caught him but I let him run through a hole in the fence"

"That rabbit sounds just like Rex. He is the grandfather and leader of all the rabbits in this area. He's also a member of C.O.F.F."

"C.O.F.F. What's C.O.F.F?"

"C.O.F.F. stands for the Council of Furry Friends of which I am a member of course. We meet in that field over there and discuss all the things that have happened, what to look out for and the things our families are going to do that week. We watch out for one another and tell each other when there are dogs and humans roaming around, so that we can hide and protect our families."

"Why do these people and dogs want to hurt you?"

"They think we are pests and that we eat their crops."

FERGAL FOX

"And do you?"

"Well only a little. We have to feed our families after all and there's more than enough to go round. Anyway Gordon I have a much more exciting and fun way of getting food"

"What's that then?"

"I wait until it is dark and then I go to where the humans live. They have things called dustbins that they throw food into and it's often very tasty. To go in the daytime is dangerous, I did it once and almost got caught. That's why I always go at night. I'll tell you what, how would you like me to take you and show you how it's done tonight?"

"That would be great Fergal. I'll need to know how to get food."

"Now, we need to hurry. It's beginning to get light. Come on, I'll introduce you to my family, we live in Tyre City."

"Where and what is that?"

"Wait and see, we are almost there."

I followed Fergal, who was ever watchful, often stopping and looking. We had to be careful there were lots of lights and I could hear the noise of cars. As we turned the next corner Fergal stopped and turning to me said.

"Welcome to Tyre City Gordon."

There was a huge mounds of black rubber rings, all different sizes, one piled on top of the other. There were big white birds standing on top of some of them. It did indeed look like a city. Fergal took me through a never-ending maze of tyres.

"Those birds you saw Gordon, were seagulls. They come from the sea just to find food. You see humans dump their rubbish anywhere and this is just one of those places, which is good for us as that means food."

We were reaching the end of the tunnel of tyres and at the end were a group of foxes of all sizes.

"Gordon this is my family."

I said hello to Fergal's family but they seemed very wary of me.

"This is my friend Gordon the greyhound – don't worry he is a friendly dog." Fergal reassured them.

There were six cubs in all and a beautiful vixen, they all gathered around Fergal. Once the family were happy that I wasn't going to chase them, they accepted me happily and I was led to a large tractor tyre where we all huddled together to keep warm. It was just like when I was a pup, with my family.

"Time to rest Gordon – keep your strength up for tonight, we will be venturing into the human's world where I will show you how to look for food in the humans dustbins".

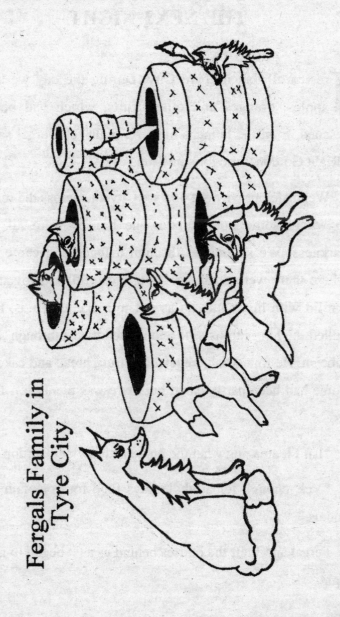

Fergals Family in
Tyre City

45

THE NEXT NIGHT

I rested all day in Tyre City. During the day we ate apples, oranges and other fruits, which had been rescued, from the humans bins. As night fell Fergal said "Right Gordon, time for some fun."

We made our way out of Tyre City and across the road to where some houses lay. The houses were all in darkness. We scrambled through a fence and came to where there were dustbins. Fergal carefully removed a bin lid with his mouth so as not to make a sound. He pulled the bin onto its side and started to sift through the rubbish. He found fish, vegetables, fruit, bread and cakes. Some had been partly eaten but there was plenty left for us.

"Isn't it amazing what the humans throw out Gordon?"

"Yes, enough for a whole days food for your family and us."

Fergal and I left the houses behind us as it begun to get light.

"We have been far too long," said Fergal as we crossed the fields.

A never ending loud, piercing sound could be heard it almost seemed to deafen us.

"Oh no" said Fergal "I am in serious danger – that's the sound of the huntsman horn. It means the hounds and their riders have picked up my scent. Look, the hounds are just over in the next field – I will never outrun them from here – I'm doomed!"

"Why, what's happening?" I asked not understanding what was going on.

"They will catch me and kill me – that's what they're trained to do. I will never reach Tyre City from here – it's too far. Oh Gordon, I've had it, I will never see my family again."

"Wait a minute Fergal – did you say they hunt by scent?"

"Yes – why?"

"Then I have an idea – let us roll on the ground together, that way your scent will be on me. I will run near to the hounds and they will get your scent on me. This will take the hounds away from you, then you can escape".

"What about you Gordon, they may kill you?"

"Don't you worry about me Fergal. I can run faster than a speeding train. They won't catch me."

"Gordon that's a great idea, are you sure it will really work?"

"Yes of course it will. I told you I am faster than a speeding train. Now quickly rub your head on my back."

The hounds were barking wildly and getting very close now. The horns of the riders were deafening.

"Right Fergal, run to the right and across that stream."

Fergal ran as fast as he could. I let the hounds get very close and hoped they would follow me with Fergal's scent on me. Suddenly there seemed to be hundreds of glowing red eyes getting closer – then I took off like a jet plane in the opposite direction to Fergal thinking, "please, please, follow me". I looked around, the hounds had slowed up, looking bemused, bumping into one another. Then they all charged in my direction. I knew I could outrun them all. As I ran faster and faster they were disappearing. I looked back when I reached a big hill – the hounds and the men on horseback had also stopped. I made my way to Tyre City tired but happy and praying that Fergal would be there. I reached the entrance it was quite dark as I made my way through the long tunnel of tyres. I then heard a loud cheer of "Hooray, hooray for Gordon" – then Fergal's six children and his wife were all hugging and kissing me. Then Fergal appeared – I was so relieved to see him.

"Gordon" said Fergal. "You are a true friend to the C.O.F.F. and you saved my life. I will introduce you to them tomorrow as a hero. Now eat this fish and fruit – we will celebrate."

I ate my meal and felt very proud of myself. I settled down, contented and fell into a deep sleep.

REX THE RABBIT

I awoke early the next day and decided to go for a stroll in the dense woodlands. I was feeling really pleased with myself when suddenly I heard a squeaky little voice.

"Hello Gordon."

I could not see where the voice was coming from.

"Look down dear boy, look down."

My eyes looked to the ground and there was the little fluffy one eared, one-eyed rabbit that I would not chase and kill on that day at my master's home.

"I'm Rex. I know Fergal Fox has told you all about me Gordon. I have heard all about you to. You were really brave in saving him from the hounds. We at C.O.F.F. (Council of Furry Friends) think that you are indeed a real friend and not an enemy of us all. I remember when I was in your garden. You could have easily caught me but you didn't. I thought then what a decent chap you were. I am an old fool sometimes, that's why I wandered into dangerous grounds where your house was and that horrible man caught me. I am so sorry I got you into trouble."

"Oh it was nothing." Gordon lied. He wouldn't forget the pain he had felt that day.

"Come. Let's go along the way together."

What an odd couple we made, there was I strolling along leisurely and poor little Rex had to work twice as hard to keep up, having to take three hops for each one of my long legged steps.

When we reached the riverbank, we rested. Rex had to catch his breath and between little puffs he spoke.

"Look Gordon" *puff* "Over there" *puff*. Rex pointed over the riverbank.

"In the corner of that," *puff* "field is where my family and friends live." *Puff* "It's called Bouncing Bottom Field."

Rex went on to tell Gordon that he was the leader of all the rabbits because he was the eldest and the most knowledgeable. There wasn't much that Rex did not know. He had lost his eye and ear when he got trapped in a poacher's snare many years ago. The snare had missed his body but Rex had stumbled with the shock, his eye hit one of the spikes and one of his ears had been trapped. Rather than wait for the poacher to return, Rex had tugged and tugged until he was free. Sadly, he had to leave his ear behind, but at least he was alive. Rex told Gordon that he would always be welcomed at Bouncing Bottom Field.

"I consider you my friend Gordon and therefore a friend of all the furry creatures. I am going to repay your kindness by telling you something I read in the newspaper, but it may frighten you so you will have to be extra careful from now on."

"What did you read Rex?"

"Well I saw this headline at the newspaper stand, over there, beyond our field."

"Where is the newspaper stand Rex, I can't see it?"

Oh Gordon, of course you can't see it from here. Only the likes of us rabbits can see it from this far. We eat such a lot of carrots which make our eyesight brilliant, we can see for miles and miles."

REX THE RABBIT

"Anyway Rex. What did the headlines of the newspaper say about me?"

"Well Gordon, young fellow, you are not going to like this. It said -

MISSING

A BLACK GREYHOUND CALLED GORDON

Big Reward for anyone who returns him

"How will they know that I am Gordon even if I am caught?"

"Don't you know? All you greyhounds have identity marks in your ears. They have letters and numbers so that the owners can identify you."

"Oh No. That means if I am caught I will go straight back to Sid, my owner, that horrible man that hit me."

"Normally you would, but today could be your lucky day."

"How's that?"

"Gordon, have you ever heard of a Rabbit's Foot being lucky?"

"No"

"Well, humans believe that if they carry a Rabbit's foot with them they will be lucky and avoid all the bad things that can happen to them."

"Is it true though Rex."

"Of course it's true."

"It seems very cruel."

"It would be if they were real rabbits feet the humans have with them, but they aren't. They are imitations made of sheep's wool."

"Oh thank goodness for that. I can't imagine rabbits running around with just three feet, let alone one ear and one eye." I laughed.

"It's NOT a laughing matter Gordon, rabbits feet ARE lucky."

I stopped laughing. Rex was deadly serious as he continued speaking.

"In my pocket Gordon, in my pocket."

He tapped the side of his little fur coat.

"As leader of all rabbits I am entrusted with the foot of STIBBAR – The King of all Rabbits. He died many hundreds of years ago and was the father of all us rabbits. His lucky foot gets passed down to the leader of the rabbits until they die. That is why I have STIBBAR's foot and it's lucky for you I have it with me."

"Will it make me invisible so that no one can catch me?"

"No, not quite. It only has certain magic powers, but you are nearly right, it can make things disappear."

"How will that help me?"

"I will show you. When I rub this rabbit's foot inside your ears it will make those letters and numbers disappear so if you are caught they will not know who you belong to. You won't have to go back to that nasty owner of yours. Now, lay down so that I can reach your head.

I laid down as Rex delved into his pocket, producing a brilliant white rabbit's foot. The magical powers shone out of it. Rex rubbed the foot inside my ear saying –
"STIBBAR THE KING OF ALL RABBITS, HEAR ME HEAR ME.
STIBBAR THE KING OF ALL RABBITS OBEY ME, OBEY ME.
STIBBAR THE KING OF ALL RABBITS, WORK YOUR MAGIC."

Then there was a strange glow about my head. My ears started to tingle, it made them twitch and itch. I had to stand up and give them a good scratch.

"Get back down here boy. Let me have a look. For goodness sake stop scratching." I did as I was asked.

"Now let me see. Ah yes, the numbers and letters have completely disappeared. Now nobody owns you Gordon."

"Thank you Rex. You are so kind"

"And so are you Gordon. So are you"

"Is it alright if I have another scratch now. Only my ears still feel funny."

"Oh, if you must. Then before I go on my way to visit my families I am going to invite you to the most important night of the Furry Friends year."

"What night is that Rex?"

"It is the meeting of C.O.F.F. (Council of Furry Friends). The night all us small animals meet and discuss what we plan for the year ahead and how to avoid the humans catching our families or us. You see Gordon, the humans don't really like us, because we eat their crops, not much, but enough to make them angry and we have to eat some of their crops to feed our families."

"Fergal, told me about the humans not liking you eating their crops and about the C.O.F.F. meeting. It sounds like a really good night Rex. Do you have food and drink just like a party?"

"Of course Gordon. After the meeting we really have fun until dawn breaks then we all go home to avoid being seen."

"When is the meeting?"

"This Friday. We meet. after dark at FUR HILL, that's just over there." Rex pointed to the right of the field.

"I'll see you there then Rex. I want to meet all your Furry Friends."

"Yes, but remember you are not to breathe a word of this meeting to anyone or else. If it does get out we could all die if the humans get to know."

"I won't tell anyone Rex. Thank you for your magical STIBBARD's foot. No one can say they own me, thanks to you. Now I am free."

Rex went home and I walked back to Tyre City, keeping my eyes open to see that no one followed me.

ARCHIE THE HARE

I was up bright and early on Wednesday morning. I knew it was this day of the week because I could hear the human voice saying it on the radio, which the farmer's son was listening to in his caravan right at the end of the Bouncing Bottom Field near Rex the Rabbits house.

The farmer's son used the caravan to stay in while the mother lambs were giving birth to their children and he looked after them until they were old enough to look after themselves. I used to watch these little bundles of white wool they looked like clouds dancing on the grass when they played with their mothers. The farmer's son, who was called Bertie, never saw me because I would hide behind the trees.

As I looked around I saw what I thought were two sticks bounding towards me. What is that I wondered? Then appeared two eyes and a big white bobtail.

"Hello Gordon" said this voice.

"Hello, who are you, and how do you know me?"

"My name is Archie Hare and Rex Rabbit is my distant cousin and he has told me all about you."

"You look bigger than a rabbit."

"That's because I am a Hare and only distantly related to Rex. Hares are bigger, also rabbits hop about, whereas hares run like mad. As I am a hare you should be my enemy Gordon, greyhounds love chasing hares."

"But Archie" I said, trying to explain that I wasn't like other greyhounds, when he stopped me and said.

"Don't worry Gordon I know you are a friend of the Furry Animals. I have been told all about you by Fergal and Rex. I would not come near you if I did not know you are our friend and it was safe to do so. Anyhow you would find it much, much harder to catch me than you would a rabbit?"

"How's that then" I said.

"As I said before, us hares run like mad and can turn very quickly. I'd rather we didn't put it to the test though as I would rather have you as a friend than an enemy. In fact, I am glad we have met so that I can invite you to our Hares Day Festival tonight."

"Is that the same as the C.O.F.F. (Council of Furry Friends) meeting on Friday?"

"Oh no. The C.O.F.F. meeting is far more important as Rex the Rabbit told you, that's where all our Furry Friends meet. Hares Day is completely different, this is the day we meet our girlfriends or boyfriends as the case may be and marry."

"Marry?"

"Yes Gordon, you see the humans have a saying *As Mad As A March Hare* that's because some of them have seen us running, jumping and turning about. We always act silly on March 1st (HARES DAY) because, what the humans don't know, is that we are so happy that we have married our partners we act silly and that is why they say *As Mad As A March Hare*. Come along tonight and join the party, although I don't think you will find a girlfriend because you are a greyhound and there won't be any of your kind there."

"When should I arrive?"

"Be at Honeymoon Heights Field after dark, and when the moon reaches the middle of that oak tree over there, that's when the fun begins."

"Where's Honeymoon Heights?"

Archie pointed to a huge field and told me how to get there. I said goodbye to Archie and promised that I would see him later that night. Archie ran off into the distance. I resisted the urge to chase him, it would only have been for fun of course. I watched until I could see him no more, then went about exploring my surroundings until I was so tired I needed a rest. I found a little nook to have a nap in and when I awoke it was already dark. I must have been asleep for quite some time. The moon was already in the middle of the oak tree. It was time to go to the Hares Day. I didn't waste any time and headed off to Honeymoon Heights Field. I had run so fast my heart was racing when I arrived. At first I thought I was the only one there, then from behind the haystacks appeared hundreds, no thousands, of hares, all with big bushy tails and long ears, all jumping about and singing.

"Gordon," a voice shouted, "Over here."

I looked and saw Archie standing next to a very magnificent looking hare.

"This," said Archie, "Is our leader Highness Hare."

Highness had the biggest ears and the longest legs you could imagine and a whopping white furry tail which was very unusual for a hare.

"Hello Gordon," said Highness Hare in an extraordinarily deep voice. "I have heard a lot of good things about you my boy and I am so glad you could come here tonight because I need to warn you about something."

"Warn me? About what Highness?"

"People are looking for you everywhere. I was outside the farmers house last night when I heard this chap called Jerome Sale on the Radio Station, BBC or something like that, he mentioned your name. I was very curious so I went to the farm again this morning and they had on the television, a man called Tim Russon was on, again speaking about you. I then happened to past the farmers boys caravan and yet again I heard your name mentioned. A girl called Ali Jones from somewhere to do with Foxes. Fox FM I think it was called. She too was talking about you.

"What were they saying?"

"Apparently you are the most wanted greyhound in the country. There is a very big reward for any person that catches you. You are a very valuable greyhound and must therefore take great care or you will be caught."

"Don't worry Highness, I am safe now, Rex the Rabbit removed the identification marks from my ears with the magic STIBBAR rabbit's foot so no one can tell who I belong to."

"Gordon, greyhounds are very valuable and the humans love them as pets because they are a kind breed, except to us furry animals, but I know you are different. At the Council Meeting on Friday we will try to come up with ideas for hiding you after we have discussed our business because, Gordon, the meeting of C.O.F.F. is so important. It is the only way us Furry Animals survive and our families rely on us leaders to make decisions on what fields to use for the year to feed our families. That's why it is so important not to let anyone know about the meeting, so make sure you are not followed. Now Gordon, enjoy the Hares Day party night."

HIGHNESS
& ARCHIE
HARE

I watched all these hares dancing and hopping, male and females all cuddling their girlfriends and boyfriends, then everything went quiet. Highness Hare stood at the top of this little mound of grass above all of them. He hopped to the right and then to the left, somersaulted and pulled his big ears right up and said.

"You will all come to me in pairs and I will pronounce you HE HARE and SHE HARE, and you will be partners and you will have children and this night, March 1st, will be your wedding day. Come forth."

It seemed to take ages as all the hares came to Highness to be married until finally the last pair got the blessing from Highness, then all that could be seen were what seemed like thousands of Furry Friends jumping, skipping, singing and dancing. They were all happy.

So this is what the humans call Mad Hare Day, only they did not know the reason why, but I did. The moon reached higher in the sky as they all disappeared. The happy couples went away to all corners of the field, joyous, happy and singing, and so I returned to my home, Tyre City. I had witnessed a truly mad but happy HARES DAY.

MARLENE MOUSE AND CAROL CAT

I was getting excited about the next night's meeting of the C.O.F.F. (Council of Furry Friends), thinking how nice it was going to be to see all my friends together and me being there. So with a bounce in my step I decided to explore the dense woods just a few hundred metres from my home at Tyre City. I thought I might find some juicy apples or plums. I liked these as they were so good for me and gave me energy. Whilst walking, I heard a very faint, squeaky voice.

"Gordon, Gordon."

I thought I was hearing things, after all if somebody was calling my name I would be able to see them, wouldn't I? So I walked on, but still this little voice kept saying "Gordon, Gordon."

I looked around once more. Still there was no sign of who the voice was coming from. I shook my head, I really was imagining things. Just as I was about to set off again, the voice, a little louder now, spoke again.

"Gordon. Down here, down here." I looked to the ground and there in the long grass I spotted the tiniest little furry animal I had ever seen.

"Hello. So I wasn't imagining things after all. You are the smallest little fellow I have ever seen. What is your name?"

"Fellow?" The little brown furry animal sounded quite put out. "I am not a fellow, I am a girl."

"Girl?"

"Yes. My name is Marlene and I am a field mouse. In fact its lucky we met Gordon because at tomorrow nights meeting of C.O.F.F. I would not have liked to be called a FELLOW, that means I am a boy."

"Oh, I am sorry Marlene. I do know the difference, I have sisters of my own, and it's just that I couldn't see you very well in that long grass. Now you are in the open, it is quite clear that you are not a fellow, but indeed a beautiful girl."

"Oh, I see. Yes. Well" said Marlene blushing, a little embarrassed by the compliment. Gordon grinned, Marlene had gone quite red.

MARLENE MOUSE

"Um. Yes. Well." Marlene cleared her throat, now was once again in control and taking on an air of authority, which again was quite amusing from one so small.

"I am the Mouse Elder and Queen of All Mice, that is why I represent all mice at C.O.F.F. tomorrow night. Now slow down Gordon, if you don't mind."

"Slow down?"

"Yes." Puffed Marlene. "Your legs are much, much longer than mine and for every step you take I need to take a hundred times more, and my neck is aching having to keep looking up at you. You are the size of an elephant to me Gordon."

"I'm sorry, I forget sometimes Marlene and your legs are so tiny. Are they the tiniest of all the Furry Animals?"

"That's right."

"Then I have a solution Marlene."

"What's that?"

"If I lay down then you can climb on my back then we can talk without having to stop for you to catch up"

"What a good idea, I'll be able to see lots of things in this forest that I have never seen before. I will be the tallest mouse in the world while I am on your back."

I laid down on the ground and Marlene scrambled up, then ran along my back until she reached my collar, which she held on to.

"Ok. I'm ready". Marlene squeaked excitedly.
I stood up as gently as I could amidst, little squeals and squeaks as Marlene held on tightly to my collar.

"Wow. This is fantastic Gordon. I feel I am on top of the world."

I laughed.

"It is quite an adventure for you Marlene. Now where do you live?"

"I live under the haystacks in the fields Gordon"

"What do you and your family eat?"

"We eat corn seeds and sometimes little worms."

"I thought you ate cheese."

"We do if we can find some, but that means a long, long trip to the estate where the humans live and that can be dangerous for us mice."

"Why is that Marlene?"

"Because the human people have cats as friends and these cats always try to catch us mice. There is one big cat who is always on the prowl trying to catch us at night."

"Who's that?"

"Her name is Carol. She is a very big cat with blue fur."

"Blue fur?"

"Yes blue fur. She is a special breed of cat. What you would call a posh cat I suppose."

"So she is your enemy then?"

"Yes. She's not the only one though. We also have to be very careful, particularly at night, as our other enemy is Jimmy The Owl. Owls are birds that live in the trees. They have BIG, BIG eyes and BIG, BIG beaks and a BIG, BIG head. Owls can see in the dark for miles they can see the smallest thing like us mice. We probably look as big as you Gordon in Jimmy the Owls eyes."

I walked on with Marlene hanging on tightly. I often felt like having a scratch as Marlene's little claws tickled me so much.

GORDON GIVING
MARLENE
MOUSE A RIDE
IN THE WOODS

I couldn't though as Marlene would have gone flying through the air, so I just had to grin and bear it.

"Are you enjoying the ride Marlene?" I asked as we crossed a small puddle of water.

"Yes, I feel like I am flying an aeroplane. I have never seen over the top of the grass before and that puddle looks like an ocean to me. I definitely feel like the Queen of Mice from up here. If only my family could see me now."

CAROL THE CAT
STALKING GORDON AND
MARLENE THE MOUSE

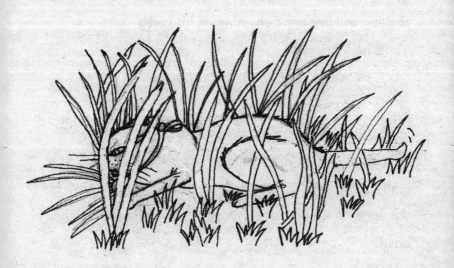

A noise from the trees disturbed them. It sounded like something or someone treading on old leaves.

"Shhhush. Listen. Can you hear that Marlene? I feel we are being watched from that tree."

"OH NO Gordon." Shrilled Marlene.

"What's the matter?"

"IT'S HER, IT'S HER." Gordon could feel Marlene shaking and her grip tightening on his collar.

"Who Marlene?"

"It's CAROL THE CAT she's after me."

"How do you know?"

"I can see her glowing eyes, she's crouched behind the long grass. I tell you I can see her eyes Gordon. She's really going to get me this time. There's no hope. I am in the open. I am doomed." A petrified, shaking Marlene, cried.

"Don't worry. I will growl at her and frighten her off. Cats are frightened of dogs."

"She's not afraid of you though Gordon."

"Of course she will be. I'm a greyhound."

"No Gordon. Everyone knows you are not like any other greyhound. You are a friendly dog and Carol knows you will not hurt her. That is why I am doomed. Can you not see her, creeping nearer."

I looked towards the noise. Marlene was right. There crouched in the long grass, getting ever nearer was the biggest cat I had ever seen and she was indeed BLUE. It was Carol the Cat and her eyes had narrowed and her tail was wagging and as she put one paw in front of the other, I caught a glimpse of her claws, glistening like sharp knives and ready to kill. I had to think quickly. It was obvious that Carol was not frightened of me, she was just feet away and ready to pounce. Without a moment to lose I said to Marlene.

"Quick Marlene. If you want to save your life do as I say. Quick as you can, run over my head, down my nose and into my mouth. Trust me."

As Carol the Cat pounced into the air, claws exposed, her mouth open and ready to kill. Marlene's little legs ran as fast as she could, over my head, down my nose and into my mouth. Crack went my jaw. Firmly closed. Carol the Cat seemed to stop in mid-air. Her prey had disappeared. I managed to run out of the way before she landed on me. Somehow Carol managed to land on her feet. She looked slightly bemused. Then she got really angry.

"Where's that mouse?"

"I don't know." I said in a muffled voice.

"That mouse has to be somewhere. She could not have disappeared into thin air."

Carol's claws were outstretched, her whiskers moving up and down. Her eyes were full of anger as she pranced and pounced in the long grass, searching for Marlene. I walked off, leaving Carol to search for the disappearing Marlene, not daring to open my mouth until Carol was well out of the way. When I was sure it was safe I stopped and opened my mouth.

"Is it safe to come out now?" Marlene called from inside my mouth.

"Mmmm." It was difficult to talk as Marlene was standing on my tongue, so I put my head to the ground and Marlene, having a quick look about, walked out, looking a little wet and untidy. After all, she had been in my mouth for some while.

"Gordon, you are so clever." Marlene said as she dried herself off. "You saved me from being killed and are truly a friend of every single one of us furry animals."

"I am so pleased I could save you. Carol the Cat is really wicked."

"There is one other thing I have to thank you for Gordon."

"Oh and what is that?"

"You saved me having to wash tonight." Marlene said laughingly. It was just like being in a warm bath in your mouth. Surrounded by all these glistening white, teeth, they shone like stars in the night."

"That's because I clean them twice a day" said Gordon "and that keeps them whiter than white."

Once again I lay down for Marlene to get on my back, when I knew she was holding on tight, I set off towards the edge of the forest. Marlene was safe and Carol the Cat had to look somewhere else for her dinner today. When we reached the edge of the forest Marlene whispered in my ear.

"I'll get off here Gordon. Thank you for the ride."

"That's ok. Glad to be of assistance."

"I'll see you at the C.O.F.F. meeting and I will tell all my family what a wonderful hero you are."

FRIDAY

I woke up in Tyre City, very excited because later that
evening, just after dark, I was going to the meeting of
C.O.F.F. (Council of Furry Friends). Seeing all my
friends together and my having the privilege of being
their guest. I rummaged through my food store, where I
found a lovely big white bone. I gnawed on this until my
teeth were lovely and clean. Finishing my morning wash
and brush up, decided I would have a run amongst the
buttercup and bluebells in the fields next to the forest, all
the time making sure I was not seen. After all I was still
being looked for by the humans, even though my identity
marks had been removed by Rex the Rabbit with the
magic of STIBBAR's Foot.

Carol the Cat, was out in the fields. I wondered if she
was still angry at not catching Marlene.

"Hello Carol" I said.

"What do you want?" Hissed Carol, her voice
sounding angry."

"Don't be like that Carol. After all. I didn't chase you did I?"

"No. I'm sorry. I didn't realise it was you Gordon. You took me by surprise."

"What are you doing here?"

"Nothing much. Just came out to stretch my legs."

"Me too. You live in Tyre City don't you?"

"Yes, with Fergal the fox and his family."

"Why don't you come and live with me?" said Carol.

"My human family are so kind and they feed me regularly and really love me. I am sure they would be pleased to have you in their home and you would not have to forage for food. You would be in the warm, taken for walks and they are really kind to animals like us."

"I'll think about it Carol." Knowing that I was quite happy with Tyre City and my freedom for the time being.

"I have to go now Carol," It was getting dark and I had to get back to Tyre City to have my dinner, which today was sausages and bones I had found in the field, left by some human people who were camping there.

"Goodbye Gordon."

"Goodbye Carol."

I waited until dark and started my journey to the field called Honeymoon Heights. I saw a light shining from Bertie, the farmer's son's caravan. That's strange. Bertie was usually in the field called Bouncing Bottom looking after the little lambs. As I got closer, making sure I made no noise because that would be the only way Bertie would know someone was outside. After all it was now very dark and as my fur was black he wouldn't be able to see me. As I got closer to the caravan I could hear other voices, so I listened to Bertie saying to his friends.

"Right my fellow farmers, tonight is the night we rid ourselves of all those pests who keep stealing from our fields. I have a foolproof plan that will catch all the leaders of the furry animals."

I had to get closer and was right beneath the window of the caravan. What does Bertie mean, I thought, and I was getting worried that my furry friends may be heading for a trap. Bertie started to talk again.

"You see" he said "my friends have laid a trap for those furry pests."

Another voice said. "How do you intend to trap them Bertie?"

"My friends are waiting and hiding in Honeymoon Heights field and when the furry leaders are all together a big net will be dropped from the trees where my friends are hiding and we will catch the lot. In fact" continued Bertie "they should be ready to drop the net any time now"

My heart started to race. I was shaking with fear. Could all my friends be caught? The only way to save my friends was for me to warn them. I ran like the wind, leaping ditches, swimming streams until I could see the field where the meeting was. The only thing in my way now was the main road, all I could think about as my heart was pounding away was to warn my friends, of the plan to capture them all. The lights of the road were in front of me, I didn't think to look left or right, my friends were in danger, I had to get to them as quickly as possible, there was no time to lose. I ran into the road, I heard a screech of tyres and a horn sounding. I stopped in my tracks just in time to see the car before it hit me. BANG! Everything went black. Then I opened my eyes. There was a terrible pain in my shoulder, but I knew I had to save my friends. I stood up and started to run off through the field to warn my friends. I could see all my furry friends gathered around the corner of the field but also the faces of the humans who had been ready to spring their traps and drop their nets and capture my friends. I gave out a loud bark and shouted.

"It's a trap, it's a trap. Run my friends, RUN."

Everyone seemed to hear my warning. The net dropped. The furry animals ran in every direction. Rex the Rabbit's leg missed the net by inches. Men running everywhere, shouting to each other.

"DON'T LET THEM ESCAPE!!!"

"Hooray. My friends had escaped and then I thought so must I, there are too many humans about. I had to get away; the men were looking for whoever gave the warning. I had messed up their plans to net and catch my furry friends.

The pain in my shoulder was spreading to my leg and I could not run anymore. I was moving slower than Marlene Mouse. My leg would not move, it was dragging on the ground. I managed somehow to get to the side of the road but could I cross it safely? My speed had saved my friends, but I was unsure if I would ever be able to run again. The pain was making me feel dizzy, I fell to the ground with a thud, everything started to go hazy, the last thing I saw was my mother and all my brothers and sisters, but this was just my mind playing tricks. I needed them now more than ever but they did not appear.

I don't know how long I laid by the side of the road but when I awoke it was dark. I lifted my head and out of the corner of my eye I could see my furry friends crowding around me. Rex the Rabbit, Highness Hare, Fergal Fox, Marlene Mouse, and many other furry animals that I had not met, even Carol the Cat. I could hear them crying and the voice of Fergal Fox very faintly saying.

"Oh, poor Gordon, he is badly hurt, we've got to help."

"But how Fergal?" said Rex the Rabbit.

"See that glass box that Gordon is laying by, it's called a telephone box."

"Yes" Interrupted Highness Hare, who was now taking charge. "I see it. We need to get Gordon help. We have to call the Emergency Service."

"We need to reach that funny thing called a telephone."

"It is too high up" said Carol Cat who was now a friend of all the furry animals, especially Marlene Mouse.

"Well," said Fergal "I will stand at the bottom. Carol you get on my back and Rex you can use your two long teeth at the front to knock the phone off then push the numbers 999 with your teeth. Marlene and Highness, you keep a look out for any humans. They may still be looking for us."

Fergal went into the phone box first then Carol the Cat jumped on his back. Rex climbed up Fergal's Fur then Carols until he was on her back. What an unusual sight they made but it worked. Rex knocked the phone off the hook and pressed 999 with his teeth. Immediately Rex could hear a voice saying "Emergency. Which service please?" But of course Rex could not talk the human language and had to leave the telephone dangling off the hook. The person on the telephone would know how to locate where the telephone box was and send help to poor Gordon.

Rex, Fergal, Carol, Highness Hare and Marlene Mouse had hidden by the hedge, along with all the other furry animals and I could see their eyes shining but full of water as they cried and cried.

"You will be all right Gordon," said Fergal.

"We will wait until help arrives. Hold on Gordon. Keep your strength up."

Just then there was a screech of breaks, as a car pulled up alongside me. A car door opened and footsteps approached me. I looked up and an elderly man was looking down at me and said.

"Hang on young fellow."

I could hear the telephone with the voice on the other end of the line still saying "Emergency. Which service?"

The man left my side and went to the telephone saying can you please send the R.S.P.C.A. as a greyhound has been knocked over by a car. Also could you contact the N.G.R.C. as they are responsible for greyhounds.

I knew my friends were hiding in the hedges and safe. All else was quiet except for the kindly voice of the old man.

"You will be all right little fellow, the R.S.P.C.A. are on their way. Just lie still for now."

IS THIS THE LAST THE FURRY FRIENDS WILL SEE OF GORDON?

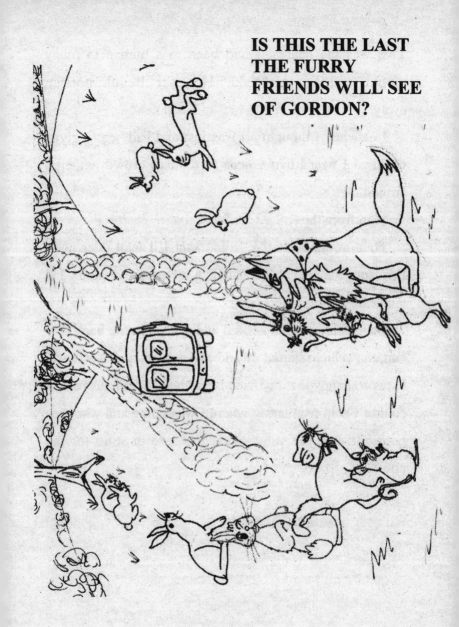

This was the nearest I had been to a human in many months and it seemed odd. However, I could not run away.

Just when I thought all was lost and had nearly given up hope I heard two voices as a small crowd gathered around me.

"I'm from the R.S.P.C.A."

Then an authoritative voice said I'll take over now. I'm from the N.G.R.C. This is a racing greyhound. I'll take care of him.

I was then carefully lifted and placed in the back of a van, the vehicle started up and as I was being driven away I was so happy that my friends had been saved, however I couldn't help wondering where I was going and who was really driving the van. What had fate in store for me now?

Thank you for purchasing The Adventures of Gordon The Greyhound. We sincerely hope that you found it enjoyable. If you have, please recommend it to your friends.

Watch out for the Further Adventures of Gordon the Greyhound

Visit Kismet Publishing Company Limited
www.kismetpublishers.com

Kismet Publishing is a small, friendly, family run company thereby retaining the personal touch that is so often lacking within larger establishments.

We pride ourselves on being an upstanding and reputable company with excellent judgement when selecting manuscripts as we have at our disposal some world renowned literary agents, one living and working for us in South Africa, plus a journalist with forty years experience under his belt! We have contacts in such places as the Far East, Australia, South Africa and the USA.

Kismet Publishing are always interested in new authors spanning all topics, so if you have written a book or thinking about writing one, please consider Kismet as we are sure you will not be disappointed in our services.

You could be just what we are looking for.